NML/CH

D1148184

NML/CH

For Sneak
and Bunny
with love, Giles

For Robert Dodd
my inspiration,
with love, Emma xx

ORCHARD BOOKS

First published in Great Britain in 2017 by The Watts Publishing Group
This edition first published in 2017

1 3 5 7 9 10 8 6 4 2

Text © Giles Andreae 2017
Illustrations © Emma Dodd 2017

The moral rights of the author and illustrator have been asserted.

All rights reserved.

A CIP catalogue record for this book is available from the British Library.

ISBN 978 1 40833 817 9

Printed and bound in China

FSC
www.fsc.org
MIX
Paper from
responsible sources
FSC® C104740

Orchard Books
An imprint of Hachette Children's Group
Part of The Watts Publishing Group Limited
Carmelite House, 50 Victoria Embankment, London EC4Y 0DZ

An Hachette UK Company
www.hachette.co.uk
www.hachettechildrens.co.uk

I love my grandad

Giles Andreae & Emma Dodd

ORCHARD

My grandad is a special man.

If I can't do it – Grandad can!

He helps me with my toys and games.

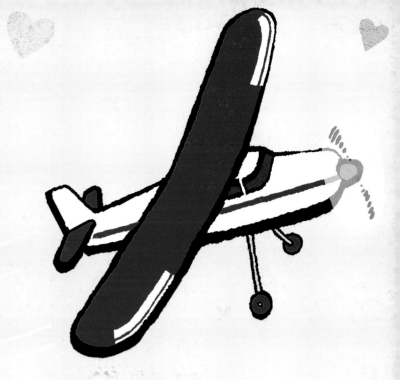

When I don't know things, he explains.

He's just so clever
and so wise,
I'm sure he'd win
the Grandad Prize!

Some days we go adventuring,

And you should hear

the songs we sing!

He likes it when
we're having fun.
He says it keeps him
feeling young.

When it's time for running races, Sometimes he pulls funny faces!

He really isn't very fast. He tries, but always ends up last!

I think my grandad's lived for years,
That's why there's hair
inside his ears.

We eat our homemade sandwiches.

Cheese in my one. Egg in his.

And if it rains, we play inside.

I make him seek so I can hide!

I drink my juice, he drinks his tea,

And tells me how things used to be.

We sometimes chat for hours, us two.

He says he loves it.

I do too.

There's so much fun
we have together.

He really is the

BESTEST EVER!